by Tim Warnes

Daddy Hug

Illustrated by Jane Chapman

HarperCollins *Children's Books*

First published in hardback in the U.S.A. by HarperCollins Publishers Inc. in 2008
First published in paperback in Great Britain by HarperCollins Children's Books in 2008

1 3 5 7 9 10 8 6 4 2

ISBN-13: 978-0-00-724909-1
ISBN-10: 0-00-724909-8

HarperCollins Children's Books is a division of HarperCollins Publishers Ltd.

Text copyright © Tim Warnes 2008
Illustrations copyright © Jane Chapman 2008

Typography by Martha Rago and Dana Fritts

Visit our website at: www.harpercollinschildrensbooks.co.uk

Printed and bound in China

For Daddy Fluff

— T.W., J.C.

Daddy **spiky**

Daddy **Fluffy**

Daddy dirty

Daddy scruffy

Daddy
GIANT

Daddy jiggle

Bouncy
Daddy

happy

giggle

Daddy busy

Daddy **strong**

Daddy *slimy*

Daddy long

Daddy
slow

Daddy
creaky

Daddy scurry

Daddy sneaky

Daddy

buzz

Daddy
bumble

Hungry Daddy

tummy
rumble

Daddy squeak

Daddy chirp

Daddy hiccup

Daddy BURP!

Daddy splish

Daddy splash

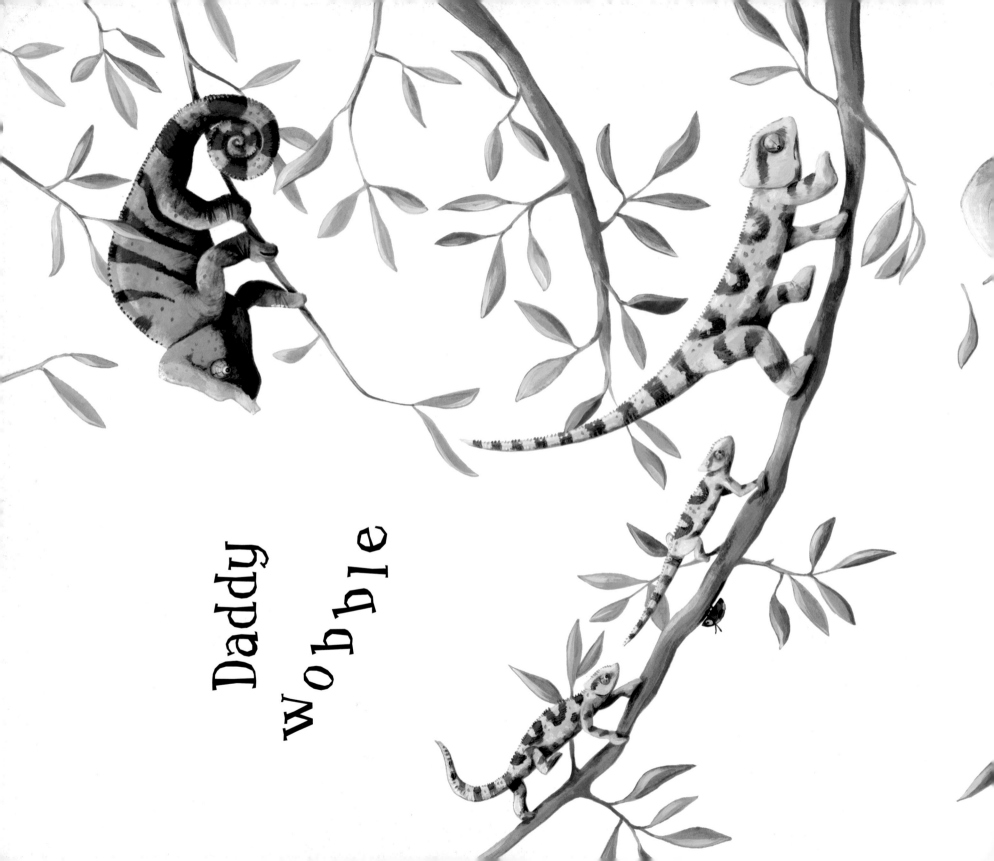

Daddy Wobble

Daddy CRASH!

Daddy safe

Daddy snug

Daddy tender. . .

Daddy
HUG!